John's Adventures
at Yellowstone Park

written by JoAnn M. Dickinson

illustrated by Daniel Wlodarski

Two Sweet Peas Publishing

Yellowstone National Park

Yellowstone National Park was founded in 1872. Ulysses S. Grant signed the Yellowstone National Park Protection Act into law, and the first U.S National Park was born!

Yellowstone National Park is huge, with an area of 2.2 Million Acres!

Yellowstone Lake is the largest lake in the park. It has 286 miles of shoreline, about 7000 ft. And it's the largest freshwater lake above 7,000 ft. in North America!

What is the difference between Bison and Buffalo? 'Bison' is the formal name of the animal, and 'buffalo' is its informal name.

Species of animals in Yellowstone since 1872 include grizzly and black bears, wolves, mountain lions, elk, bison, pronghorn moose, and big horn sheep.

Grizzlies are still present in Yellowstone Park. They grew from a population of 136 to 728 grizzlies between 1755 and 2020.

Wolves were entirely eliminated by 1926, but they were re-introduced to the park in 1995.

John and his family are leaving bright and early for **Yellowstone Park** for a new adventure!
The family can't wait to get there and learn everything there is to know about the park. Each of them has chosen a few favorite sights they want to see.

John wants to become a Junior Ranger, and Dad wants to visit **The Grand Canyon of Yellowstone.**

Mom is interested in exploring Grand Prismatic Springs and 'Old Faithful.' And John's sister, Emma, wants to see the volcanic mudpots bubble, hiss, and boil.

John tells his dad, "We'll need to ask a park ranger how I can become a **Junior Ranger.**"
His dad responds, "Okay! When we arrive, we'll ask them for all the details."

After Dad stops at the park entrance,
John peers out of the window,
telling the park ranger,

"Today, I'm going to become
a Junior Ranger in
Yellowstone Park."

The park ranger hands John
a map and a pamphlet about
the Junior Ranger program.

Dad announces,
"Our first stop is the Fountain Paint Pots!"
It's where we'll see hot springs, mudpots, geysers, and
fumaroles, which are also called steam vents.

He continues, "Did you know they're the hottest places in the park? Their temperatures are hotter than boiling water! Geysers explode with steam and hot water. How do I know all this? I've been watching videos about it on the internet."

As they arrive, John jumps out
and runs down the boardwalk...
stopping near a small pot of mud
that is bubbling and hissing.
Dad shouts, "Wait for us!"
as the roaring sounds get louder.

Dad explains, "The hissing is caused by gases including steam, **carbon dioxide**, and a little **hydrogen sulfide**. Those gases rush up from under the Earth through the open vents."

The **bubbling mud** looks so exciting that
Emma says, "It looks like thick, chocolate milk,
but I would never want to drink it!"

As they walk back to the RV, Mom declares, "Our next stop will be the Grand Prismatic Springs, Yellowstone's largest hot springs. They are the most visited hydrothermal features in the park."

When they get there, Mom shows John and Emma how the beautiful, bright colors and the turquoise blue water glisten in the sun.

She reminds the kids that the water is extremely hot, so they should always stay on the boardwalk. The water travels 121 feet from a crack in the Earth to reach the surface of the spring.

Mom asks, "Did you know this is the third largest spring in the world? The Grand Prismatic is 370 feet in diameter, 360 feet long, and 160 feet wide!"

The hot spring has bright bands of orange, yellow, and green rings in its deep waters.

The multicolored layers get their hues from different species of thermophilic (heat-loving) bacteria living in the progressively cooler water around the spring.

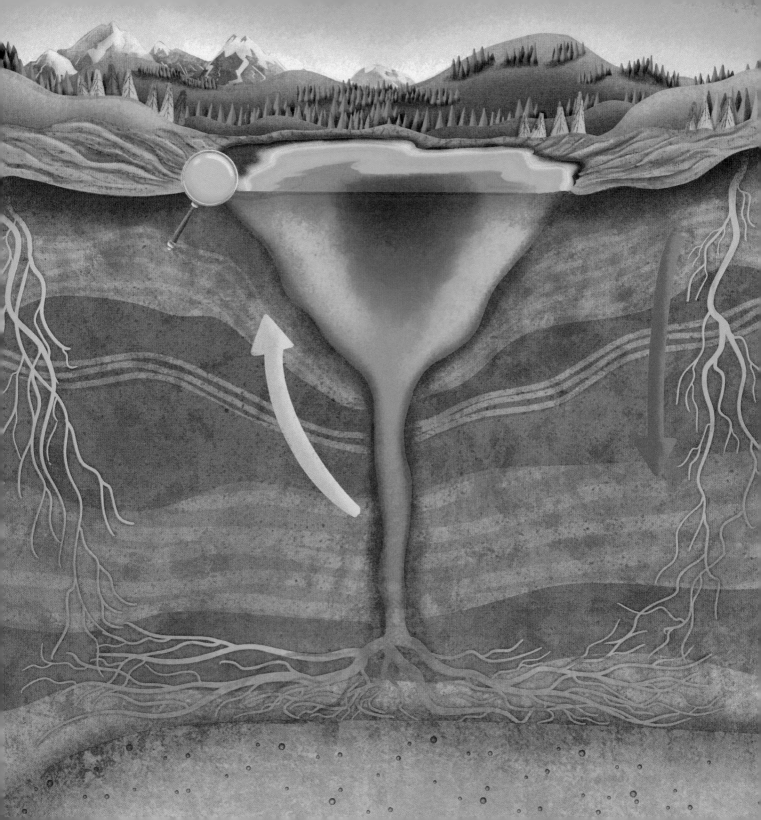

John asks his dad, "When will we get to Old Faithful? That's where I go to become a **Junior Ranger.**"

Dad reassures him, "It's our next stop. Did you know it's the most **active volcano,** located right below our feet? It may not be the largest, but it's known to be the most active."

"And do you know what makes it so active? Water percolates through hot fractured rocks."

On the way to Old Faithful, John and his sister spot a bison nearby, they declare, "That's the largest animal I have ever seen!"

Dad reminds them, "Many wild animals live in the park—including brown bears, grizzly bears, elk, pronghorn moose, and big-horned sheep. We need to stay mindful of the danger they pose."

Soon, they arrive at the Upper Geyser Basin, where Old Faithful is located. It's where John becomes a Junior Ranger, having completed all the listed activities:

First, he visited with a ranger.

Second, he hiked on a park trail or boardwalk.

Third, he completed the activities in the booklet to learn about park resources, crucial issues, and concepts like hydrothermal geology, wildlife, and fire ecology.

"Look!" shouts John.
"I received my badge, and now I'm a **Junior Ranger!**"

Mom and Dad are really proud of John
because of his **commitment**
to becoming a Junior Ranger
and reaching his goal so quickly.

After they leave Old Faithful, Dad calls out,
"Finally! Here's the sight I've been waiting for
'Grand Canyon of Yellowstone.'

I've read that this area is better known as the **Upper and Lower Falls**. Let's go take a look at the amazing views!"

Together, the **family hikes** up
to the top of the falls,
looking across the ravine
to the other side.

Emma points and exclaims,
"Look! Way over there,
I see another **waterfall**.
The people look as tiny as ants!"

Dad explains,
"That's Artist Point,
also called the Lower Falls."
We will see that view of the
waterfall next!

As they start hiking down
to the Lower Falls,
John and his sister peer over
the edge of the rock wall.

John can't believe how steep
the waterfall is. He's amazed
at the beautiful rainbow
he sees at the bottom!

It has been a very full and exciting day. The family has enjoyed visiting the Yellowstone Park wonders.

They have been fascinated by all the sights and plan to visit the **Upper Loop of Yellowstone Park** tomorrow.

They can hardly wait!

A few intriguing terms:

Fumaroles, or steam vents, are the hottest hydrothermal features in the park, with temperatures above those of boiling water.

Geysers erupt with steaming hot water. Variations of each geyser's underground reservoir determine whether or not it is regular and predictable like Great Fountain Geyser in the Lower Geyser Basin or irregular like Giant Geyser in the Upper Geyser Basin.

Mudpots are acidic features with a limited water supply. Their consistency and activity vary with the seasons.

Upper Geyser Basin, home of 'Old Faithful,' is the most active volcano below your feet. It's not the largest, but it erupts more often than the other giant geysers, making it the perfect place to visit during a trip to Yellowstone. Each eruption prediction is based on the last eruption, so times vary by the day. The interval between eruptions can range from 50 to 127 minutes. During eruptions, the water temperature typically measures 204 degrees. The eruptions expel up to 8,400 gallons of boiling water that can reach a height up to 184 feet!

Yellowstone's Twenty-Seven Associated Native American Tribes:

Among Yellowstone's twenty-seven Native American tribes are: Blackfeet, Gros Ventre, Salish-Kootenai, Crow Apsaalooke, Northern Cheyenne, Nez Perce, Shoshone-Bannock, Eastern Shoshone, and Northern Arapaho—to name a few from Montana, Idaho, and Wyoming.

About the Author

JoAnn M. Dickinson is a multiple award-winning and best-selling author. This is her seventh self-published book but she's not stopping there. New this year, will be The Lou's Zoo Series, Rylee Series, A National Park Series, and more on the way.

Follow JoAnn's author journey at www.JoAnnMDickinsonAuthor.com

Other books available:

About the Illustrator

Daniel Wlodarski is a creator of children's book illustrations; book covers and is an animation artist. He lives in a tree house with his wife, two sons, and a daughter. When he is not drawing, he is floating on a tire swing, dreaming about what clouds taste like and holding his breath. Visit Daniel's website, danielwlodarski.com.

Made in the USA
Las Vegas, NV
22 April 2024

89006929R00024